Robert Louis Stevenson

# THE MOON

*Pictures by*

Tracey Campbell Pearson

FARRAR STRAUS GIROUX

NEW YORK

Distributed in Canada by Douglas & McIntyre Ltd.
Color separations by Embassy Graphics
Printed and bound in China by South China Printing Co. Ltd.
Designed by Robbin Gourley
First edition, 2006
10  9  8  7  6  5  4  3  2  1

www.fsgkidsbooks.com

Library of Congress Cataloging-in-Publication Data
Stevenson, Robert Louis, 1850–1894.
    The moon / Robert Louis Stevenson ; pictures by Tracey Campbell Pearson.— 1st ed.
      p.   cm.
    ISBN-13: 978-0-374-35046-8
    ISBN-10: 0-374-35046-9
    1. Moon—Juvenile poetry.   2. Children's poetry, Scottish.   I. Pearson, Tracey Campbell.
  II. Title.

  PR5489.M57 2006
  821'.8—dc22
                                                    2005040067

For Mom

The moon has a face
like the clock in the hall;

She shines on thieves on the garden wall,

On streets and fields

and harbour quays,

And birdies asleep in the forks of the trees.

The squalling cat and the squeaking mouse,

The howling dog by the door of the house,

The bat that lies in bed at noon,

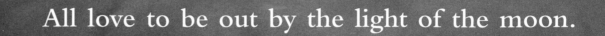

All love to be out by the light of the moon.

But all of the things

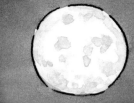

that belong to the day

Cuddle to sleep to be out of her way;

And flowers and children close their eyes

Till up in the morning the sun shall arise.

The moon has a face like the clock in the hall;
She shines on thieves on the garden wall,
On streets and fields and harbour quays,
And birdies asleep in the forks of the trees.

The squalling cat and the squeaking mouse,
The howling dog by the door of the house,
The bat that lies in bed at noon,
All love to be out by the light of the moon.

But all of the things that belong to the day
Cuddle to sleep to be out of her way;
And flowers and children close their eyes
Till up in the morning the sun shall arise.

—Robert Louis Stevenson, "The Moon"
From *A Child's Garden of Verses*, 1885